"Love more everyday."

This book belongs to:

Dedication

To my late parents, Marie Georgette and Arnold
Paul: Without your sacrifices, I would not be here.
Thank you for showing me how to love.

I Am Not Being Lazy I Just Don't Understand

Written By
Gina PauL

iLLustrated By
DG

Printed in the United States of America
ISBN-13: 978-1-7344789-0-7

Published by Gina Paul
New York, NY
Library of Congress Control Number: 2020908235

Special Thanks

To my siblings (Magda, Edwige, Lesly, and Woodley), my brother-in-law Waldeck, my sisters-in-law Natalie and Mercy, my sister-friends, my cousins, my aunts and uncles, my church family, and all my nieces and nephews: Thank you all for allowing me to run my mouth while still showing me love and support.

Chapter 1

As I was walking into my new classroom for the first time, I felt more afraid than I've ever felt in my life, fear that almost overwhelmed me. My hands were sweating, my legs were shaking, and I was afraid that everyone could hear my heart beating like a drum in my chest. The children in the classroom stared at me with big, curious eyes. I stared back with fear and confusion. I was fearful that I would not be understood, nor would I understand what was being said. It puzzled me that I had been placed in a classroom where no one spoke my native language of Haitian Creole.

As I walked to the last available seat at the back of the classroom, I felt everyone's eyes on me. I now understood how bugs feel under a microscope. "Welcome, Georgette, to class 5-10," said the woman whom I assumed was the teacher. I looked up at her standing in front of the classroom, but all I understood was my name.

At that moment, I wish that I could go back to my native country, where I did not have to worry about starting my education all over again by learning the alphabet, numbers, shapes, and basic words in a new language. I wanted to wish myself back to Haiti, where I felt safe and where everyone spoke my language.

Moving to a new country was not my idea; I did not have a choice. One day while eating dinner, my parents announced to my siblings and me that we were moving to a new country soon, to a big city. New York City, to be exact— the Big Apple, they called it. They did not explain why.

I was very sad because that meant I was leaving my friends and extended family behind, but I was also excited about a new adventure.

My parents told us about the tall buildings and bright lights. They also told us about the trains that ran underground very fast. That sounded a little scary, but I still wanted to see and experience it. I wondered how they made the buildings so tall; I'd only seen buildings taller than four stories on television. My parents explained to us that some of the buildings were as high as one hundred stories. *Wow*, I thought, *I don't think that I will be able to see all the way to the top of those buildings.* I was curious about how the trains were able to run under those buildings without the buildings falling on them.

Later that night, while in bed, my siblings and I talked about what we were looking forward to doing once arriving in New York City. We were very excited to try new foods and meet new people. I am very talkative and love meeting and talking to new people. Unfortunately, in my excitement, it never occurred to me that I would encounter a language barrier.

Throughout the first week of school, everyone in class was working and talking around me. However, no one tried to speak to me except for the teacher, whom I still did not understand. I tried smiling to see if that would encourage the kids to approach me, even to say hello, but they looked away as soon as we made eye contact. I was hoping that if they smiled back, then maybe I could approach them, but no smiles. I felt confused and alone even though there were twenty-seven other people in the classroom. It felt like I was on a deserted island.

Chapter 2

The first few days of school, whenever we left the classroom, the teacher would say, "Georgette, come," as she made a motion with her hand for me to follow along with the class. She used that way to communicate with me when we had to go to recess, gym, and the cafeteria. Unfortunately, my first time in the cafeteria was not a good experience. I followed Mrs. levy, that was the name of the teacher, to the cafeteria, as she led us to a table and then just left.

I was completely lost. I did not know what to do. So, I followed the class, sat down, and waited.

The cafeteria smelled and sounded very different than what I was used to at lunchtime back in Haiti. It was loud, chaotic, and confusing. The children were laughing, going from table to table, and being playful with each other, and some even shouted things across the room to each other. Back in my country, each class was served family style on a picnic-style table. We were able to have conversations; however, our voices were not supposed to exceed a certain level. We were not allowed to leave our tables unless it was to go to the restroom, or else we would get in trouble. It was the complete opposite here. I wished someone had prepared me for what to expect.

I was hungry and nervous, but I simply did not have the words to ask what we were supposed to do about lunch; therefore, I sat there and kept waiting. It seemed like forever before I saw a woman with an apron on and a net on her head walked out of the kitchen and called out, "Class 5-09, get in line." An entire table full of students got up and formed a line where the food was. By the second time that the lady came out, I realized that she was calling each table to get in line in order to get food.

I observed the kids once in line to see what they were doing so that I would know what to do when my table was called. When the lady with the apron looked at my table and said, "Class 5-10, your turn. Get in line," I waited until most of my class lined up before I followed them. I was very nervous about eating the food because I had no idea how it was going to taste. Since arriving to the United States a little over a month ago, prior to starting school, my mom had only cooked food from my country; therefore, I had not had the opportunity to try any new foods yet. I hoped that lunch tasted good.

When it was my turn to get food, the lady behind the food counter asked me, "You want french fries, hon?" I did not understand what she was asking me, so I said, "yes," which was what the student before me had answered when the lady had asked her the same question. The lady placed some long, fried, light brown food—what looked like cut-up potatoes—and five circular, fried dough-like pieces of food on my tray.

As I made my way back to my seat in the corner, I smelled the food on my tray a little to see if I could make out what any of it was. I hoped no one saw me and thought I was being weird. After sitting down, I took small bites just in case I didn't like them. I realized that I was right: the light brown food was potatoes. I later learned from one of my siblings that the circular, fried dough-looking food was called chicken nuggets. I had never seen chicken or potatoes served like that before, but I liked them.

For the first few days, lunch was not bad. We had french fries, chicken nuggets, burgers, pizzas (which I loved), and beef patties. However, on the fourth day, we were given something meaty and mushy that the lunch ladies placed between two pieces of bread, called a sloppy Joe. I did not like it at all. I saw some kids eating peanut butter sandwiches, but I did not know how to ask for that; therefore, I did not eat lunch that day.

The lunch period was boring and lonely. It would not have been so bad if I were sitting with a friend. However, I always sat alone at the corner of the table, watching the kids talk, laugh, and eat in groups.

Chapter 3

Two weeks has passed and not much had changed in the cafeteria or the classroom. I still sat in my class full of people yet felt lonely and sad. I'd picked up a few words, but not enough to communicate. The teacher was teaching, the kids were working, talking, and even having fun, but I felt like a square peg trying to fit in a round hole. Mrs. Levy tried helping me, but nothing she said made sense. Everything that was written on the chalkboard seemed foreign to me. I knew and understood most of the letters; however, there were some letters like the letter Q, which does not exist in the Haitian Creole alphabet, that made it very challenging. The letter sounds were different in English; therefore, I could not sound out the words like I would have in my native language. I felt like I didn't have a voice.

While sitting in class, I overheard a couple of the students and teachers use the word lazy while looking at or pointing at me. I heard, "She is being lazy" a few times. I did not know what the word *lazy* meant, but from their facial expressions, it did not sound good. I asked my mom about it one day.

"Mama, what does 'she is being lazy' mean?" I asked her while sitting in the kitchen having a snack.

"It means when someone doesn't want to work," my mom answered.

I was shocked. *How can they say that about me?* I thought. *They do not know me or what I am capable of. Not only do I want to work, I want to participate and make friends. They have no idea how hard I've tried to figure out what was happening in the classroom or other places in the school building.*

I was so upset that the students and teachers thought that I was being lazy, I could not even finish my snack, even though I love ice cream.

The next day in class, I wanted to shout at everyone that I was not lazy; I just did not understand the language. I wanted to show the kids that I was just as smart and capable as they were. Speaking a different language did not make me less intelligent or a lazy person. I just needed to understand what I was expected to do. If someone was able to translate for me and I were allowed to write in my native language, I would have shown them what I was capable of doing.

One morning, on my way to school, I decided that I would find a way to participate in class. All morning, I tried figuring out what exactly I was going to do or say. When I finally did, I was excited but nervous. I decided to ask one of the groups of girls who were working together if I could join them.

When we separated into small groups, I decided to make my move and ask them if I could join their group. I leaned over to them and asked, *"Mwen ka chita avèk nou?"* which in English means, "May I sit with you?"

11

The girls looked at each other, then at me, and started giggling. Feeling silly, I straightened back up in my seat and looked forward while they continued to giggle. I felt embarrassed and wanted to cry, but I was determined and was not going to give up.

On my way home that day, I realized that maybe they had laughed because they did not understand me. Therefore, I decided to learn the phrase in English.

When I arrived home, I wrote down the question in my native language and used an English/Haitian Creole dictionary to translate the sentence to English, word for word. Then I asked my family to help me pronounce the words to the best of their knowledge, since they also were learning English.

Feeling confident, the next day I leaned over to the same group of girls and asked, "I sit to you?" I was very proud of my English; I had practiced pronouncing the words all morning. However, this time the group of girls laughed out loud, banging their hands on their tables, holding their stomachs, and slapping their knees. The teacher had to eventually quiet them down. *What did I say wrong?* I wondered, scratching my head.

For the next couple of days, I tried hard to figure out what I had said wrong. I repeated the phrase in my head over and over again. I had translated it just like I say it in my own language, but something was not right.

Chapter 4

On the third day, I waited until after the class separated into small groups and approached Mrs. Levy, in hopes that she would help me figure out the correct sentence. As I walked up to her desk, everyone stopped working and stared at me because I had never approached the teacher before. I was frightened but determined.

Mrs. Levy seemed surprised to see me but had a small, inviting smile on her face, which made me feel a little more comfortable about approaching her. "I sit to you?" I said to her as I pointed to the group of girls. At first, she seemed confused. She looked at the girls I was pointing to and then looked back at me with a frown on her face. Then she asked me, "You want to join them?" while pointing at the group. I repeated the phrase, "You want to join them?" three times in a whisper, just low enough for me to hear.

I ran back to the girls and, with a huge smile on my face, loudly asked them, "You want to join them?" The whole class started laughing. I looked around, wondering why they were laughing. I said the phrase just like the teacher did. I knew that my pronunciation was not perfect, but I thought that it was easily understood. Sighing, with my shoulders sagging in defeat, I went back to my seat, embarrassed and upset. I folded my arms across my chest and hung my head. My face felt hot with embarrassment.

After the teacher had quieted the class down, she came and squatted down in front of me. She asked me, "You want to learn how to say, 'Can I join you,' right?" I did not look at her or responded because I only understood some of her words. She stood up and motioned with her hand for me to follow her.

I really did not want to, but with a sigh, I stood up and followed her. She led me in front of the same group of girls. I refused to look at any of them; I had my head down and my hands hanging loosely at my sides, staring at my shoes. Slowly, Mrs. Levy said, "Can I join you?" I did not know what she expected from me; therefore, I ignored her. She repeated the phrase again and said, "Now you," pointing at me.

I looked at her and shook my head. I knew she wanted me to do something, based on her body language, but I was not sure what it was. She said the phrase again, pointed to me and said, "You repeat." In the past couple of weeks, I'd learned the meaning of that phrase. I realized that when teaching the class new words, the teacher would say a word, then say, "You repeat," and the whole class would first repeat, then spell the word.

Although I did not want to be ridiculed again, I repeated the phrase anyway. Mrs. Levy said, "Bravo!" and started clapping. Some of the kids clapped, as well. I lifted my head and started smiling shyly. One of the girls pulled my chair closer to theirs and said, "Come join us" while motioning with her hand for me to come. I felt overjoyed as I walked to my chair and sat next to the girls.

A few days later, I decided to make new friends. Feeling brave in gym class one afternoon, I decided to approach one of the girls while we were waiting for our group's turn to play volleyball. She was sitting by herself, so it felt safer approaching her than approaching the girls who were sitting in groups. I thought that if she rejected me, at least it would not be done in front of others.

I was so nervous that my palms started to sweat, and my breathing became a little faster. I walked over and sat down next to her on the bench. I pointed to myself and said, "My name Georgette," then pointed to her and said one of the new phrases that I'd learned: "What is your name?"

The girl looked at me, smiled, and said, "My name is Tessa." Just then, the gym teacher blew his whistle for our group to start our game. I was very happy that I had been brave enough to make a connection. It was not a leap, but it was another small step to making friends.

Chapter 5

Within the next few weeks, school got a little easier. I started to interact more with my classmates by pointing to an item in the classroom and saying the name in Haitian Creole. One of my classmates would then tell me the name in English. When I wanted to learn how to say *"chèz"* in English, I touched the shoulder of the girl who sat to my right, whose name was Lea. I pointed to the chair and said, *"chèz"*; she looked at me and said, "chair." I repeated the word three times in a whisper in order to memorize it. I had realized early on that if I said words or phrases at least three times, I had a better chance of memorizing them.

After a few days of pointing and learning, however, I could tell that my classmates and even the teachers were getting annoyed with the constant interrupting and pointing. During math, I saw the boy to my left, whose name was Alex, with a *kalkilatris* in his hand, and I wanted to know the name in English. I reached over and waved at him to get his attention. When he turned towards me, I smiled at him and asked, "This, *kalkilatris?*" while pointing at it.

Alex rolled his eyes, sighed loudly, and said, in a very annoyed voice, "Calculator." Then he turned away from me, shaking his head. That was not the first time that someone had gotten annoyed with me when I asked for the name of an object. Feeling discouraged, I decided to stop asking for help.

After three months in school, things were progressing, but not as fast as either the teachers or I would have liked. I was still not comfortable expressing myself in English. I was still using body language and hand signals combined with some new sentences that I'd been learning in order to communicate. Some of the students did not like working with me. I overheard them say that they did not believe that I would be able to contribute to the assigned projects due to my heavy accent and unfamiliarity with the English language.

During science, Mrs. Levy assigned us partners to work with on a project to construct a homemade lava lamp. My partner's name was Lizzie. The teacher gave us all that we needed, including written directions on how to make the lava lamps. I was excited to work on the project because I had always loved science. Back in my native country, I've always gotten high grades in my science classes.

My partner, however, was not very excited. She groaned when the teacher told us that we would be working together. "But I can barely understand her," she complained in a whiny voice. That frustrated me a lot, because I had much to contribute. If I knew the language better, I would have been able to show her and the other students. What they did not realize was that I understood a lot more than I was able to express. Although we were able to complete the project with the help of Mrs. Levy, I was not happy with the way that Lizzie treated me.

After the winter holiday break, I did not want to go back to school. I was tired of people being frustrated with me and calling me lazy. Although some of the kids would say hello and even tried having conversations with me, they got frustrated quickly when I had difficulties responding clearly enough in English. By February, it was I who was frustrated with them. No one at the school seemed to realize how difficult it was for me. Hearing words and not understanding their meaning is scary and frustrating. For a ten-year-old, it felt like I was on a bicycle going down a hill with a brick wall coming at me fast, and I had no breaks.

Chapter 6

Two weeks into February, a boy from my country was transferred from a different class into my classroom. He had come to the United States the previous year. Although he was not fluent in English, he spoke and understood enough to translate for me. What a relief. The first phrase that I asked him to teach me was, *"Mwen pa parese, mwen jis pa konprann."* It took a couple of minutes, but I got it.

The next time a student called me lazy, I looked her in the eyes and said, with my heavy accent, "I am not lazy, I just don't understand." She rolled her eyes and walked away. It felt good that I was able to defend myself, thanks to the new boy. His name was Arnold, and he was very helpful. It felt great to have someone who I could relate to, someone who I knew wouldn't laugh at my pronunciation and jumbled-up sentences. His English was not so great either, but it was much better than mine. He was lucky to have had a Haitian classroom aide in his class the previous year, who turned out to be a major help to him.

During English Language Art one day, we were given five words and were asked to make five complete sentences using them. The words were: *expand, population, guardian, donate, and introduce.* I knew what population meant, but the rest were new to me. I decided to start my first sentence with the word *population*.

Alex had been moved from the desk to my left in order to make room for Arnold when he joined our class; therefore, I was able to move closer to him to get help. I knew the sentence that I wanted to make with the word population. In my head, I created the sentence in Haitian Creole, then translated it in my broken English. I wrote down: *United States is large population Haitian people.*

I showed it to Arnold, who then helped me to correct it. "You are missing a couple of words to make it a complete sentence," he said patiently. "In front of *United States* you need the word *the,*" he corrected. "Also, you might want to replace the word *is* with *has,*" he suggested, and continued until we completed the sentence.

With gratitude, I made the corrections. My new sentence read: *The United States has a large population of Haitian people.* We continued on like this, with Arnold explaining what the words meant, me writing the sentences the best that I could, and Arnold helping me to correct them. He was a very patient friend.

With Arnold's help, I was able to engage in short conversations with other kids and the teacher. By April, I was able to use the sentences that I was learning to make new friends.

Chapter 7

During springtime every year, the school put on a spring dance for the fourth and fifth graders. I heard several of my classmates talking about it, and Arnold told me that he had attended the previous year and that it was fun. I had never attended a school dance before, but it sounded like fun.

Two weeks before the dance, I asked my parents if I could go. Reluctantly, they agreed, but only because Arnold's mom was chaperoning. The next day, I was very excited to tell my new friends in class that I was going to the dance. Tessa and I had gotten close in the past couple of months. When I saw her as I entered the school building, I excitedly told her about my news. "Tessa, Tessa," I called out loudly, "I go to spring dance."

"Really?" she exclaimed, just as loudly, with a huge smile on her face.

"Yes," I answered, smiling back. We linked arms in the hallway as we walked to our class, making plans about what we were going to wear.

Even though I was more comfortable speaking English with Arnold, I was still able to communicate with others in and outside the classroom. I did not allow my heavy accent or the fact that some of the kids still laughed at my mispronounced or misused words to stop me from talking, participating, or making new friends. Making my own small group of new friends was a huge plus for me. At lunchtime, I now sat with Arnold, Tessa,

and a boy named Sam. I felt like I was part of the laughing, loud, and playful group of kids in the cafeteria. The feeling of belonging was in every smile and laugh.

By the end of the school year, I felt like I had gone through a battle and won. I was not yet fluent in English, but I was able to do well enough in the class to graduate and move on to the sixth grade. On graduation day, I felt like I was riding a bike on leveled ground, on a sunny day, with a cool breeze blowing and my eyes closed, knowing that I had made it through my first year, and it felt great!

Discussion Questions

- What would you have done to help Georgette succeed in the classroom?

- Have you ever felt left out?

- Have you or any of your friends ever ignored another child on purpose?

- What are some ways that children can bully others?

- Do you have children from other countries at your school?

    - If yes, have you tried making friends with them? If not, why not?

About the Author

Gina Paul is an inner-city early childhood special education teacher and will soon be a licensed bilingual teacher. She came to the United States at the age of ten and spoke no English. She learned the language through watching educational children's programs on television. Gina is a strong believer in bridging the gap between cultures and communities, which she believes can be accomplished by educating young people about history, creating opportunities to share stories, recognizing individual differences, and having a healthy appreciation for diversity.